SERENDIPITY

Published By

Serendipity

Edited By Riswana

Published by: Poetry World Org.

Publisher's Address: Haryana

Printed under PWO in India

Edition : I (2022)

ISBN (Paperback) - 9789390724901

Book Design by POETRY WORLD

POETRY WORLD ORG 2022

SERENDIPITY

AN ANTHOLOGY BY PWO

INDEX

8

Beril Jebastin

BLESSING IN DISTRESS

As soon as the ambulance stopped in front of the hospital, Tina got out of it and with the help of two other nurses, she took her mom inside the hospital, running along with the stretcher. The doctor arrived and her mom was immediately taken to the ICU.

Tina couldn't wait outside. She wanted to rush inside the ICU and be with her mother to see what was happening to her. Tina lost her father when she was a child and it was her mother who fulfilled her needs and took care of her.

The doctor came out of ICU and said Tina that her mom was alright. He told her, "I am indebted to your mom."

Tina stood in shock and confusion. "You may not be knowing me but I know you and your mom very well. She was my tuition teacher. You were a kid at that time. I know how she worked hard to raise you. She was my ray of hope. She gave me the courage to pursue my exams without fear, which is one of the main reasons I am a doctor today. It is time for me to repay. Don't worry. She will be alright"

Tina thanked God and her luck for being with her.

Ankita Sarkar

LIFE

In the middle of life,

Where there is little hope,

All we have to decide is what

To do with the time that is given to us,

But I being poor, have only my dreams,

Your brains in your head.

You have feet in your shoes.

You can steer yourself in any direction

You choose,

You are on your own.

It is a far better thing that I do,

Than I have ever done,

It matters not what someone is born,

But what they grow to be.

Juliet Hudait

MOTHER

Who is a mother?

The person who sacrifices all her happiness?

The person who gives up all her dreams because of you?

The person who guides you towards success?

Or all of the above?

Various types of mothers exist

Some sacrifice career!

Some sacrifice sleep!

Some sacrifice self love!

And some sacrifice passion!

The one who teaches how to love,

The one who teaches how to fight for what you believe in,

The one teaches how to care,

The one who teaches how to respect,

Is a mother!

Caring, Loving, Graceful, Passionate!

Oh! There aren't just enough adjectives in the

dictionary to describe a mother!

Mother - The Goddess in human form,

We love you forever.

Yasir Ali Durrani

LOST IN YOU

Is It Me Or Is IT You

My Mind Entangled With The Notion Of You

Is My Mind Poisoned Or Is It Blessed

Wondering the Wonders Of Your Tenderness

Shall I Admonish My Mind Or

Shall I Acknowledge Your Entanglement Or

Shall I Neglect Your Entanglement

Lost In You

Like A Peculiar You Are To Me

Or Is It Just Your Faddy Tenderness

Shall I wonder Around This Maze Or

Shall I Avail This Moment Too

Entangle Myself More Deep In To Your Notion

Is My Mind Poisoned Or Is It Blessed

Komarraju Keerthana

EVERYTHING IS WORTHY

In this world, nothing is futile.
The artistry of our hands turns anything into
worthy.

So, never think yourself as worthless..
Instead stream in edifying yourself and meet your
hidden notability.

Uma Dabburi

TO MY SERENDIPITY LOVE

While I reposed in a ragged shell, fevering with fury on this prejudice world I found you.

Notwithstanding substantial financial in my 30's, I was outgrowing my age. A man in early 30's looked withered like a man in early 40's. The endless struggle to success was sucking my youth from within. Love and dating and relationships, I have given up long back on them. How could I not? I didn't have energy for myself and to give a supplementary part of me to another human being seemed nonsensical.

One afternoon, as I was reverting to my office, I bumped into her. She has managed to paint my entire white shirt brown with her decaf. At that instant, I was unknown to the miracle she is going to shower my life with. The following day I noticed a pretty girl waiting in the lobby. It was late and I was returning back home; someone knocked me from behind, "Excuse me, my apologies for yesterday. Would you like to have dinner with me? My treat."

As these words poured out of her mouth in such simplicity, I was drawn to her. Years passed, we talked, we fell in love, we married, and life could not be more pretty. She was my serendipity. I was not expecting her but she ushered into my life and beautified it.

To my Serendipity Love.

Siba Shankar Sahoo

USELESS

Some said that I'm useless

Yet they used me

Some said that I'm a great guy

But still didn't choose me

Some loved me with a heavy heart

And left me loosely

Some treated me as their enemy

So, they kept me closely

So, if you ask me why I am hurt

And why do I lose sleep

It's because of the scar I got

For loving those people...

Who always used me mostly.

Mr.V.Heymonth Kumar

LOVE AT FIRST SIGHT

We met with an accident,

That made us to this incident:

We started to love one another,

This embedded us with the feather;

I cannot stop the holy love

On her soul which does give

Life to all the living beings here,

I wish to live with her anywhere!

It is nothing to feel bad,

I want to be her child's dad;

I cannot do my most needful duty,

Her eyes intoxicate me by her beauty.

Anwesha Rath

My journey

I start my drive

From your eye

To your nose

The fragrance of your body

As a rose

The ears

Becomes my dears

And the juicy lips

Just give the feeling to kiss

Seeing the smile

It changes my style

The hand I hold

Become I soul

Walking together

Becomes my nature

This is the journey

Which always in dreams I meet

And I want to repeat

Serena Ahluwalia

AN ARTIST'S ODE TO THE CANVAS –
THEIR MASTERPIECE

I'm lost in the Blue,

While you lie in wait.

My thoughts are filled with you,

Even though the lines aren't straight.

It's hard to see you blank.

It's even harder to see you stained.

You are the one, I want to swank,

'Cause this side of me is unrestrained.

I perceive the world in You,

'Cause you're my drug, my Elixir.

The way I express my point of view,

My rapture in the depth of your Texture.

I start with petals, but end up with Thorns,

Choose bright hues but shift to the darker Ones.

Will I be able to do justice to the Seasons,

Choose passion instead of Reason?

You're impatient to be labelled as a masterpiece,

And here I am pondering over the difficulties.

I know every time I promise,

But it won't be long before you find Solace.

When you're at the pinnacle of success,

Feeling your artist's caress.

N.Abitha

LOVE IN ABSENCE

Love Lost

It was road to my School

Gang of friends chatting about last period

It was Boys who watch every step

First it was insecure

Watching, turned to be mutual

A fair boy tall height

Charming voice wavy hair

Used to feel him as mine

Slowly fell deep in love

Next day his absence made me long

Came early to school to search him

He passed away bike hit him

Said the other boy.

Christina Angel. J

WINGS

Journey started my wings are ready to fly

My destination visible and feels to fly high

Need to make a magical decoration on sky

It's my path, my wish, my heart, only mine.

Suddenly the chains locked my legs,

My wings are shaking and seeks,

They want me to take up the forbidden - marriage.

But I really discouraged when thy feel as - courage.

No need to claim the down hill.

Where you never feel a shill

Being stable on my vision.

That's the thing my mind taking revision.

Conveyed my thoughts on my strong No's

It's prospect way I ever knows.

Broke my chains front of folklores.

Now I could fly where my victories.

Jeevitha.S

STUPENDOUS NIGHT VIEW

Her mind was filled with lots of chaos,

She lost her hope on things and felt low.

When she looked up at the sky,

She was awestruck by the view

When she observed the scenario of around her,

She understood the betterment behind things.

She realised that happiness depends upon how we

conceive things.

She saw the enchantress even un that gloomy sky,

Even the unilluminated nights shows exquisite in

its own way,

Stars glinting as diamonds in the dimness,

The crystalline aerosphere expliciting peace,

That stupefying glance made all her torments

evanesce,

There exists the glide of positive vibes.

She summoned more wisdom and insight,

All her dejections flew away;

And her eyes once again shimmered with jubilance.

Blessita. A

GO BEYOND INFINITY

Merlin and Serah are siblings. They love to live in their own world. Merlin's world is realistic with challenges and she had no faith in magic, fantasy and so on, whereas Serah lived in a world of magic. On a fine day after dinner both decided to play in balcony. The view from their balcony was majestic with billions of stars. They stood quietly watching all the stars.

All of a sudden Serah shouted "SISSY... LOOK IT'S A DOLPHIN!!!" Merlin looked up in boredom. She hated the so called "world of magic" that Serah lived in. It didn't impact her in anyway.

"Sissy..." Serah whined, "Do you see the dolphin in the sky?"

"Dolphins can't-" Merlin was cut off and shocked. Serah shook her. Merlin looked at the sky; she was astonished and said, "Ow!!!"

"Can you see it, can you see it?" Serah shouted with excitement.

Merlin looked up again in frustration; preparing to prove her little sister Serah that, "There is no way-" she stopped again. She paused as she stared at the dolphin in the sky.

"See?" Serah looked smug and jumped up and down, "There is a dolphin!!!"

Merlin was like "But how…? It can't be… "- she was shocked. And said to herself that, "There is no way this is real" and pinched herself.

"Why can't this be real?" Serah asked, and was utterly confused.

"Dolphins can't fly," Merlin vocalized calmly.

"But your imagination can," replied Serah.

It was a pleasant surprise (Serendipity) for Merlin.

Moral: Younger sisters too can teach us valid things. Your limits are somewhere up there, waiting for you to reach beyond infinity.

Srija Sadhukhan

MAGICAL RHYMES

Alice in wonderland was a dream

In a rabbit hole of whim,

Of some magical rhymes

In the story of fairy times.

Those stars look like fairy lights

In the darkness desirous sights,

Riding on the rainbow with an unicorn

At the head having magic horn.

Watching the sky changing magical hue

As everything seems perfect in fairytale land of

blue,

Flying high with feathery wings like free parakeet

Diving in the ocean of feeling experiencing magical

heat.

Muralidhar Bansal

BEGINNING

New beginning is a clarion to your new life that all your sadness and failures are left in the past so that you can compete in the present in a better way.

Each step, life gives us a new beginning like adulthood from childhood, parenthood from adulthood, thereafter old age. These stages develop learning for the next generations.

New beginning has some tensions, anxieties and worries. But one cannot become a warrior unless s/he handles the worries.

New beginning makes the days and night a means for horrible dreams. But we also can't dream of becoming knight without the nightmares.

Devanshi Shah

IT'S LIKE

It's those moments,

Those tiny moments, locked in my heart,

That never let me sleep without my heart smiling.

It's like you came and swept away my pain

Your kind and beautiful heart gave me a reason to

smile,

Even in my darkest of hours,

You are the one whom I think about.

It's like my heart and soul starts doing symphony

I felt like I am Bewitched by you,

In a way, I could never express it by my ink

You became the reason my words turn into a poem.

This serendipity is what I have always dreamed of

Now when it's turning into reality

My words seem to fail me,

But my heart smiles more often now.

Roselynn Saud

MY YOU

I know I'm still journeying towards unearthing

your Existence.

I don't know how long it's gonna take but it's

Worth it, I know.

You don't have to be perfect, I merely hope you

accept me with my scars.

I only wish you adore my imperfections.

No! I don't need a man with muscles,

I just want him to have warm arms adequate to

embrace me.

No! I don't expect him to buy me all the souvenirs,

I just crave for him to be a boon to me forever.

No! I don't long for him to take me around the

planet,

I just ask him to be the centre of my Cosmos.

No! I don't want you to strive to be the best edition

of yourself, particularly for me,

I just want you to be there by my side in my highs

and lows.

I just want you to realise that my heart and soul is

eternally yours and will always be.

Together we will nurture this tremendous voyage

of life till death knocks on our door.

A small perpetual vacancy in your generous heart,

to abide for eternity is only what I ask for.

Sadia Shahab

A SPLENDID ACCIDENT

A person with the body of pearls;

entered in my vague life with flowers.

Our eyes collided in a peculiar moment,

my heart mumbled "this is the top bestowment"

I don't know his intention, why he came for?

I never felt those bizzare feelings before.

He stole my time and I made him mine,

he said "he can't love me" and my word was "fine"

I started loving him like nobody could ever,

he answered on my feelings tore my heart like a

paper.

He returned and left me with some birds flying

above,

that was my very first curious accidental love.

Glady. A

LET ME LOVE YOU

Must every love start from a romantic day?

It wasn't a rainy day.

I was in a miserable state.

After delivering the package

My mind started delivering it's questions,

What's next in life?

With thousands of confusion

I started my ride

Eyes met with a sparkling smile.

The next minute I found myself in pain

I speculated it's gonna be another vain.

But the warm smile melted my coldness

Bringing back all the boldness.

To crush my curse,

And prove the power of will.

That smile was the only thing,

I had to feed my soul.

Little did I know,

That smile earned many hearts.

The thought of not owning it

Made me a living dead person.

But then I realized at a point,

The smile has its own heart.

So, I chose to stand out, to see the warm smile.

After all, it is the Serendipity of my life.

Abia Esther P

NATURE THE HEALER

Fascinated by his charms,

Inquisited of how it feels

To be wrapped by his arms.

His ambience reveals

The Creator's innovation.

His bright self

Is many men's inspiration.

Long rides alongside him

Makes my heart swim

In the pool of glee.

Mountains - my kind of obsession!

V. Vinusha Subha Harini

THE LOVE LEFT UNSAID!

It was pitch dark outside and there was no moon neither stars to be seen. Seema was in a dilemma whether to confess to her long love Kirsch. Kirsch was the handsome hunk of her high school and it happened that only she didn't mind him. Seema was so aware of herself that no handsome man would want her. So at the first sight she ignored Kirsch who was irresistible.

Kirsch was a handsome man with zero knowledge and was quite arrogant. Sometime as a punishment the teacher would ask him to sit with Seema. He would try to distract her or talk to her, even though Seema notices all his antics and inner smile, she would face palm herself openly in front of him and scowls at him. This made Kirsch impressed because it was the first time for a girl to ignore him. But it wasn't love, of course no one would love a girl like her.

She was perfect by character but flawed in beauty. But Seema being optimistic and bold girl was never bullied nor talked behind. Kirsch would sometimes sit beside in her class. Then came the time of the exams and her heart skipped a beat. It was because Kirsch wanted to study with her and he was so close to her while studying.

Seema began to fall in love unknowingly but she knows he won't love her back. Thus, she decided to hide her feelings and continuously scowl at him. This made him more curious and as he was arrogant he wanted her to fall for him. So he acted so cute and childish around her alone. Later they both found their paths and remained friends.

Now Seema wasn't able to hide anymore because they both spend so much time together. Thus, she decided to confess to him tomorrow and she was getting ready to get rejected. On the other hand Kirsch also felt the same but he wanted her to say it.

The next day, Seema dressed cutely, and picked up the Lavender bouquet that she bought for him. She texted him to meet her by the cliff. She wanted it to be romantic as well as challenging so she chose the mountain cliff. He was so surprised but also he was exited as he was waiting for this moment. He guessed that she'll confess to him. As he climbed up the cliff, he saw a woman dressed in Purple and holding a Purple bouquet.

He came closure and was just a step away from her. That woman was none other than Seema. He was completely taken aback by her beauty, yes she had put on some make-up. The greenery and she in Purple looked as if she was the flower of the whole mountain. Seema said "I know you won't like me but I have to confess it to you, I Love You and I've always wanted to say this to you Kirsch."

With those words she fell off from the cliff. Kirsch wasn't able to understand for a moment what happened because it all happened so suddenly. When he realized the love of his life was not there but dead. He cried his heart out and stopped being a human thereafter. He turned cold. His Love was Left Unsaid! He loved her dearly... She became his everything who took away his everything with her. Now he wanted her to come back and waited hoping that someday she'll return.

Kamlesh Singh

THE JOURNEY OF MISS X FROM FLIGHT PARTNER TO MY SOUL MATE

As soon as I boarded my flight, I took the window seat and resumed reading my novel. It was "the girl at room 105" by Chetan Bhagat. I was so into his book that I didn't notice a pretty face taking the seat beside me . I loved reading and aspired to be a writer.

As the air hostesses started giving their customary instructions, I noticed the girl sitting beside me having a novel in one hand and her purse in another.

I, who had never initiated a conversation with a girl, felt my heart racing, however, I was more interested in the novel that the pretty girl was holding.

After a while, I noticed it was "The missing 54" by Chander Suta Dogra, an author who inspired me a lot.

The flight took off. Both were busy in their novels. The curiosity of mine won over my fear. I began the conversation.

X - Sorry to interrupt but a Chander Suta Dogra fan?

ME - Not a fan but yeah, I love some of his books. What about you?

X- Oh yeah, I am a big fan. Read all his novels.

X - Good for you. May I know what you are reading?

Suhas - Oh, it's nothing. It's a book gifted to me. It's a love story.

X - Sounds interesting. So, do you like reading?

Suhas - I do. I love reading. I must have read over 100 novels. I want to be a writer one day.

X - So, which novel is your favourite?

Since the conversation was about novels, both of us were involved. We were discussing novels ranging from Chetan Bhagat to Ajay K Pandey.

The sound came. It was announced that lights will be switched off. They realized the plane was going to land but they continued to talk about novels. As the flight landed and X was about to leave, I stopped miss x. It was so stupid of me. I told,

"I don't even know your name. How about we exchange our novels and leave it there?"

Miss X winked at Suhas, gave him her novel and took the novel from him. Without saying anything, miss x left, taking her bag. I was sitting there, wondering how I could miss such an opportunity.

As I was waiting for taxi in the airport, I opened the novel given by her. I opened the page she was reading, where her bookmark was placed. As I lifted the bookmark, I realised it was her business card with all the contact details. Her name was written in bold Sameera.

Few years later, when I was standing at an event releasing my first novel, I opened the first page of my novel, the name Sameera was again written on bold, this time as an acknowledgment by me, Suhas thanking my loving wife for the support.

In all the talks about the novels, somewhere our story also began.

Mridul Jain

FEAR

The greatest fear in this world is,

Not to face the fear,

And what the world says you hear...

Be strong when you face your fear,

B'coz it is real not reel life my dear...

Being in your fear, make you always rear,

You have to face the fear, to be your own dear…

Overcome your fear, over your life my dear,

B'coz it's only one life my dear.

Ishita Banerjee

MY DEAR BROTHER

You stole my food

But we're never once rude

At times you yelled at me

To get back on my feet

At times you willingly

got scolded on my stead

You protected, defended

also made fun of me

But you always were

The best brother, you ever could be

Where can I ever find, a bond so pure?

A person who'd always be by my side

I've never been more sure

You're the best gift from God

That I've ever got

My one & only dear brother

I love you a lot.

Sara S

OPEN WIDE O' EARTH

See ye Comrade, the core explodes

I know your disbelief, cross all its odds

The dust, the flames, through Pripyat bridge

Passed on to the air, flown over the edge

The sound of the reactor, the light it gave

Was just a start to the truth- a handful it save

"It is all the reactor's fault, not mine", says Legasov

Now the city is a graveyard, you see as I saw

The width is not new, nor the hole and dust

Few years back, an "American Revenge" shown the

crust

To cities of Japan and shouted- Open Wide O'

Earth

Countless dead in a snap of time, but ones has no

growth

Then a fifty on spot and a fifty yet to save

Let the night be over, so the numbers left come by

day

I'm sure Comrade you and I will die very soon,

But not before Chernobyl doomed and begone.

K.Monisha

தேசம் மீது நேசம் காண்போம்

உதிரம் சிந்தி, உயிரை விட்டு

உயரம் சென்ற தலைவர்களாளே

நாம் காணும் சுதந்திரம்..

விதைக்கப்பட்ட உயிர்களுக்கு

விழுதுகள் விளையும் நாள் இதுவோ!

உறைந்த உடல் உன்னதமடைய

உட்குரல் கொடுத்து உதவும்

உன்னதப்படைப்பு இது...

அமைதி என்னும் ஆயுதம் ஏந்தி

அகிலம் ஆண்ட

ஆளுமைகளுக்கு அனுதினமும்

வீரவணக்கம்....

உதிர்ந்த உயிர்களுக்கு

உதயம் காணும்

உன்னத நாள் இதுவே....

விடுதலை காற்றுக்கு

விலை கொடுத்து

விண்ணைத் தொட்ட

வீண்மீன்களுக்கு வீரவணக்கங்கள்.

உதிரம் விதைத்து

உயிரை காக்க

உயரம் பறந்த

உள்ளங்களுக்காக

உற்சாகமாய்

உறுதியளிப்போம்

தேசம் மீது நேசம் காண்போம்!

Navaneethakrishnan S

கண்ணில் என்ன பிழையாம்

என் வழியெல்லாம் உந்தன் நிலைதாம்..

கண்மறைவில் என்ன நாடகமாம்...

என் நினைவெல்லாம் உந்தன்

முகம்தாம்...

கெட்டது ஒன்றும் யாருக்கும் நான்

நினைத்து பார்த்ததில்லை...

தனக்கென வாழும் இவ்வாழ்வில்

மறந்து உன்னை

நான் வாழ்ந்ததில்லை....

நீ என்னுடன் இருந்தா பரவாயில்லை...

வேறொன்றும் இவ்வுலகிலே எனக்கு

தேவையில்லை...

N.Priya Darshini

என் இனிய தோழியே

கருமேகங்களில் இருந்து அழகிய துகள்கள் போல

சிறு துளிகளாய் என்னை வந்து தீண்டும் பொழுது

நான் காற்றை போல மென்மை ஆகிறேன்

சிறு சிறு துளிகளாய் என்மீது சொட்ட சொட்ட

நானும் மயிலை போல சிறகு விரித்து;

கூச்சல் இட்டு நடனம் ஆடுகிறேன்

உன்னால் தான் இவ்விடமே அழகு மலரை போல்

மென்மையாக காட்சியளிக்கிறது

ஆதலால் நான் மெய்மாறந்து போனேன்னடி

அந்த வானத்தில் இருந்து இவ்விடம் நீ வரும் பொழுது

என் கண்களில் மட்டும் ஏதோ ஒரு தேவதை தென்

படுகிறது.

Sreejini.M

கடின உழைப்பு

இரவும் பகலும் இணைந்திருப்பின்
இரவில் மிளிரும் விண்மீனின் அழகும்
பகலில் ஒளிரும் கதிரவனின் அழகும்
கண்ணுக்குப் புலப்படா -
அதுபோன்றே வெற்றியும் தோல்வியும்
பிணைந்திருப்பின் நெற்றியில் மறைந்திருக்கும்
நம் முயற்சியும் தோல்வியில் ஒளிந்திருக்கும்
நம் முயலாமையையும் எவர் அறியக்கூடும்?

Prateek Gaurav

शाम-ए-अवध:लखनऊ

दुनिया में मशहूर तो बहुत सी चीजें है, लेकिन हमारी शाम-ए-अवध कुछ खास है,

कैसर बाग की दिन की सादगी से, बीबीडी की शाम की नजाकत तक,

मशहूर मिठाइयों की दुकानें हो या भूले भटके चौराहे यहाँ हर किसी का अपना एक नवाबी अंदाज है,

इसीलिए तो कहते है! दुनिया में मशहूर तो बहुत सी चीजें है, लेकिन हमारी शाम-ए-अवध कुछ खास है,

चिनहट, मटियारी और कपूरथला की गलियों-गलियों में शोर होता है और भाई साहब यह अमीनाबाद है, यहाँ हर एक चीज पर मोल-तोल होता है

पलकों-पलकों कितने मौसम हमने निकाले है घंटाघर ने सब देख डाले है,

बदलते हुए मौसमओं के साथ घंटाघर ने देख डाले सारे बदले हुए नवाबी अंदाज है,

इसीलिए तो कहते है दुनिया में मशहूर तो बहुत सी चीजें है, लेकिन हमारी शाम-ए-अवध कुछ खास है,

तहजीब,नजाकत और नेशनल पीजी पूरे देश में लखनऊ की आन और बान है,

तो वहीं जनेश्वर मिश्र पूरे एशिया में देश की शान है,

पत्रकारपुरम और 1090 की शाम, और हर टाइम

पॉलिटेक्निक और वेलिंगटन में लगने वाला ट्रैफिक जाम

ताज होटल और यूनिवर्सिटी की रौनक और चौक का माहौल,

यही सब बातें गोमती रिवरफ्रंट को बनाती कुछ खास है,

इसीलिए तो कहते है दुनिया में मशहूर तो बहुत सी चीजें है,

लेकिन हमारी शाम-ए-अवध कुछ खास है,

रूमी दरवाजा,रेजीडेंसी और सारे पार्कों में घूमने जरूर आना,

लेकिन गुफ्तगू थोड़ी धीरे करना भूल भुलैया में,क्योंकि

इमामबाड़ा में तो दीवारों के भी कान है,

पढ़ाई में तो हम सबके बाप है, लेकिन तहजीब में पहले आप है,

वह गोमती नगर का नजारा है इतना प्यारा कि कोई खुद को

कहते हुए रोक ना पाए कि यह लखनऊ शहर है हमारा,

दिल है लखनऊ का हजरतगंज,और वहाँ की धड़कन है उसके आशिक

और यहाँ पर लोग अब आशिकी कम गनजिंग ज्यादा करते है

और गनजिंग अंग्रेजी का एक नया अल्फाज है

इसीलिए तो कहते है दुनिया में मशहूर तो बहुत सी चीजें है,

लेकिन हमारी शाम-ए-अवध कुछ खास है||"

Aditi Sachdev

तीसरी लहर.. सोचना जरूर...

त्यौहार हमारी जिंदगी में फिर से आनंद-उमंग ला रहे है,

पर क्या हम सब फिर अपनी जिम्मेदारियों से मुँह फेर रहे है?

सोचना जरूर...

हाँ, हम सभी को खुशियाँ मनाने का अधिकार है,

हाँ, हमारे मन में एक दूसरे के लिए अटूट प्यार है,

हमारे जीवन में खुशियाँ लाते यह त्यौहार है,

पर हम क्यों बार-बार दोहराते गलतियाँ हजार है?

सोचना जरूर...

अभी कुछ महीनों पहले ही अपनो को हमने खोया,

उनके जाने पर हमने ही पहाड़ जैसे दुखो को ढोया,

हाँ, त्यौहार है, मानना है रस्में जरूरी,

पर जिनको खोया उनके सपने छोड़ ना सकते अधूरे,

फिर क्यों हम वही गलती करते है?

क्यों गलतियों से हम सीख नहीं पाते है?

सोचना जरूर...

पहले की गई भूलों से हमें सीखना होगा,

नहीं तो फिर हमें उसी तरह दुखों को भोगना होगा

कर्तव्य पथ पर चल, क्यों ना अपनी जिम्मेदारी निभाएं,

स्वयं के साथ दूसरो को भी उनका फर्ज समझाएं....

सोचना जरूर...

Arslan Beg

धैर्य

क्यों मन को विचलित करता,
     तू निराशा को इंगित करता,
तू धैर्य रख और साहस कर,
     चल अपने लक्ष्य चिन्हित करता।।

तू शीघ्रता को छोड़ दे,
     मन को तू अब विराम दे।
रख धैर्य अपने जीवन में,
     अब विचारों को आराम दे।

त्याग ही वो शक्ति है,
     जो जीवन तेरा सफल करे,
तू धैर्य रख और प्रयास कर,
     त्याग, दुर्बल को प्रबल करे।

असफलता का सफलता में परिवर्तन, धैर्य है।।
नीरस जीवन के सरस होने का कारण, धैर्य है।।
क्षण भर की शीघ्रता से उत्तम है तू धैर्य रख,
तेरी इस विडम्बना का एक ही निवारण, धैर्य है।।

55